# Mini-Stories

*A Free Woman and Weary and Tare*

## Maleigh

**Outskirts Press, Inc.**
**Denver, Colorado**

This is a work of fiction. The events and characters described herein are imaginary and are not intended to refer to specific places or living persons. The opinions expressed in this manuscript are solely the opinions of the author and do not represent the opinions or thoughts of the publisher. The author has represented and warranted full ownership and/or legal right to publish all the materials in this book.

Mini-Stories
A Free Woman and Weary and Tare
All Rights Reserved.
Copyright © 2009 Maleigh
v4.0

This book may not be reproduced, transmitted, or stored in whole or in part by any means, including graphic, electronic, or mechanical without the express written consent of the publisher except in the case of brief quotations embodied in critical articles and reviews.

Outskirts Press, Inc.
http://www.outskirtspress.com

ISBN: 978-1-4327-2982-0

Outskirts Press and the "OP" logo are trademarks belonging to Outskirts Press, Inc.

PRINTED IN THE UNITED STATES OF AMERICA

# A Free Woman

Calvin Steele is a successful business man who comes to the small town in Chicago on business and falls for a beautiful woman, who slips right through his hands. He's crushed.

Londa Reece is a Child Advocate Attorney. She has a best friend who falls in love with her brother Elliot. She has issues with not supporting her boyfriend and his career.

Mack Allen, he's a cheating, lying husband, whose with a different woman almost every three to six months. His infidelity finally causes his wife to leave him for good.

Elliot Malcolm is an Attorney, who represents his best friend in her divorce and falls in love with her.

Patrice Allen is the faithful and meek wife of Mack Allen. She is the "Free Woman"

Destiny Ross, she is the mistress to Mack Allen, whom he becomes engaged but never gets married to her.

John Shaw is the boyfriend of Londa, who has a successful career and is best friends with Calvin.

Patrice and Mack have a fight over his infidelity.
Mack and Patrice are an Upper Class Black couple, who have martial issues.

Patrice: Who is that tramp you've been sleeping with Mack?
Mack: You mind your business. I'm the man where your bread is buttered on!
Patrice gets in his face.
Mack: Patrice, I don't have to explain to you any of my dealings with any of the women I talk to.
Patrice: Who is she? I saw the damn condom wrapper! You are nothing but a liar and a cheat!
He grabs her and pushes her on the bed.
Mack: Don't talk to me that way!
Patrice fights to break away from him.
Patrice: Let me go.
He has her pin down on the bed.
Mack: Calm down Trice.
Patrice: I'm sick of this.
Mack lets her go and starts to pack his bags.
Patrice: Where are you going?
Mack: Don't question me woman.
Patrice: Fine! Get the hell out! I don't need you.
She pulls her shirt up that was falling off her shoulder. She goes into the kitchen in the back foyer of the house. She

sits at the table and sob.
Next, the front door slams.
Patrice gets on the phone.
Patrice: Londa!
Londa: I'm on my way!

Moments later.

Patrice and Londa at Patrice's they sit having a pow-wow about Mack who just betrayed her (Patrice) trust. Patrice has a glass of Chardonnay. Londa hates Mack and she and Patrice have a disagreement about if she takes him back.
Patrice: Okay Londa, I hear you but I'm not listening. I hate him for what he's done.
Londa: I told you that Mack was a two timer. He was with Destiny and her sister.
Patrice: And I took him back after I found out. I know….I know, I'm the one whose a fool not him.

Londa: This is Mack's 4$^{th}$ time making a plum fool out of you.
Patrice: So what do you want me to do?
Londa: Get a divorce. He keeps hurting you.
Patrice begins to sob. She realizes that Mack will never change.
Londa: I say divorce the bastard.

Mack, meanwhile, is laid up in bed with Destiny. They relax in her condo lightly dim with candles and soft jazz music playing. The condo he is paying for.
Mack: I missed being away from you.
Destiny: Me too. You've been away from me too long. 3 weeks is too long for me. I have to get mine.
They cuddle up closer.
Destiny admires her engagement ring.
Destiny: So, what are you going to tell Patrice?

Mack: You let me worry about that.
Destiny: So are you moving back in.
Mack: Yes, In do time.
She kisses his chest and makes her way down to his belly button. She then straddles his love.
Mack enjoys the moment of intimacy and ready for round two.

Later.

Londa and Patrice sit and have ice-cream. Londa always seem to comfort Patrice.
Londa: John and I were supposed to go out tonight but I canceled, so I can be with my friend.
Patrice: No don't cancel your date, invite him here. I'll be on the phone with my attorney anyway.
Londa looks at her in disbelief.
Patrice: Call your man girl.
Londa: Okay….no, I feel bad because John will be here and you will be by yourself. No!
Patrice goes in the hot tub. She picks up her phone and calls her attorney.
Patrice: Hello Elliot. Can I meet with you tomorrow? I'm going to go through with it this time. I need a lawyer not a brother figure. I'll see you tomorrow bye.

Londa orders Chinese food. Patrice slips on a pair of jeans and a tank top.
Patrice: Well, everything is all set. I really think I can go through this.
Londa: John called and he insist on seeing me tonight. I told him about what happened. The good thing is that…(looks at Patrice's expression). He ran into a old college buddy and wants to bring him by.
Patrice gives her a strange look.

Londa sets the table in the kitchen.
Patrice: Okay, my heart is suppose to be broken but I don't or I can't cry anymore.
Londa: Because, this has happened more than once and you are used to the lies and deceit. Do you think Mack will come back tonight?
Patrice: That fool has only been here for a few days, he's with one of his whore's I'm sure.
The door bell rings.
Londa: That should be John or dinner.
Patrice: I'll grab some wine.
Londa opens up the door to see a fine tall, dark and handsome chocolate man. Standing next to him is a white or bi-racial male. He is tall with smooth hair and a nicely trimmed gotee.
Patrice: Who is it? (She peers through the door and sees the light skin fella and John.
John and Londa is busy locking lips until Patrice clears her throat.
Londa: Sorry.
Patrice: Hi John…
John: Hey Trice, you look good. (gives her a hug). Sorry about Mack. Oh and this is my old college buddy Calvin Steele.
Patrice: Hello, nice to meet you.
Londa: I ordered our favorite Chinese food.
Patrice: Come in.
Calvin is memerized by Patrice's beauty. She is of a smooth shade of caramel with a short spiked hair-do. Londa is just the opposite, she has a light complexion with long hair.
The Chinese Food arrives shortly.

They sit and have dinner.
John: Calvin and I go way back to our college days, we are going hang out and….

Londa: (buts in) Yes, but I wanted to spend my QT with my man.
They laugh.
Londa: So Calvin, tell us about yourself.
Calvin: I like Chinese food. I own my on Advertising Business and I promote my products around the world.
Patrice interjects.
Patrice: Which is?
Calvin: clothing but mostly luxury car products.
John and Londa gulp down there food, so they can go and spend some QT.
Londa: Okay. John and I have to catch up.
Londa and John leave the room and go out on the patio.
They get into a red hot kiss. John starts undressing Londa. They go into Patrice's sauna and get into some red hot sex.

Calvin and Patrice in the kitchen. Patrice gets nervous because, Mack could come home any minute. She gets up and clears the table.
Calvin admires her every move.
Calvin: Tell me about you.
Patrice: you don't want to know about me.
Calvin: Yes I do. He gets up from the table and helps her clear it off.
They walk into the nook area to talk.
Patrice: want some more to drink?
Calvin: yeah but only if your drinking with me.
Patrice: Of course.
They sit down admiring each other for a moment. There eyes meet every once and a while. Patrice has not been laid in 2 months. She always had an excuse or Mack was never home. She checks Calvin out and then he breaks the ice by asking her to show him where to find the bathroom.

Patrice: Two doors down to the right, down this hallway.

She starts pacing the floor for a while. She sees Londa's shoes on the patio floor and she knows what's up with her and John.

She gives off a smile and gets back to Calvin, who is still in the bathroom. She sneaks off to make a call. Patrice wants to get hers but that is much unlike her.

Mack answers.

Patrice: Where are you?
Mack: That is none of your business.
Patrice: Oh it isn't…uh, you know that your pathetic. I want a divorce. I had enough of your lies!
Mack: Is that all you have to say.
Patrice: Don't bother about coming home tonight?
Mack: I'm busy.
Patrice: Okay. (hangs up) She sobs.
Calvin hears her. She is standing in the hallway with her back to him.
Calvin: You okay.
Patrice: yeah! She pulls it together.
Patrice: Look, I'm not feeling well maybe you should…
Calvin: Okay. He leaves and doesn't press her with any questions.
She goes into her bedroom and locks the door.

Calvin walks to the front of the house. He sees a wedding photo of Patrice and Mack. He looks down the empty hallway. He calls for a cab and goes back to his hotel. He is living at a hotel until his house is ready.

Londa and John finish up.

Londa sees two empty glasses on the table.
John: You don't think.

Londa: no. I'll check in the back room. She walks over to Patrice's bedroom door. Trice…. Trice you in there.
Patrice: yeah.
Londa: You okay.
Patrice: Yeah. Can I just be left alone, I'm not feeling well.
Londa: Okay. Look, I'm going to set your alarm okay and I'll see you tomorrow.

The next day.

Patrice gets dressed up, she puts on her best dress and pumps with her $800 bag across her shoulder. She is going to see her attorney in style. She drives off in her convertible two door Lexus.

Londa calls her.

Londa: Hey you, how's it going?
Londa at work at her firm.
Patrice: I feel good today. I'm about to be a free woman this time.
Londa: you okay. Calvin has been calling John all day asking about you.
Patrice: He doesn't know anything about me.
Londa: Maybe, he wants to get to know you, so I invited him to my place tonight along with my best friend.
Patrice: If you are trying to match make its not going to work.
Londa: You need to get Mack out of your system once and for all because….
Patrice: Londa please! I'll go.
Londa: Good, I'm cooking. We are having shrimp scampi, broccoli sprouts and smothered potatoes.
Patrice: I'll bring tums.
They laugh.
Londa: Later.

They hang up. Patrice gets out of her car to meet her attorney. She feels like a brand new woman today …a free woman. She meets with Elliot.

Elliot: Hey girl! You look damn good. If you weren't like a sister to me.

Patrice: Who would know? I haven't been laid in a two months want to try me.

They chuckle.

Elliot: (watches her strut in front of him) Let's get down to business.

Patrice wants to be validated again.

Elliot: How much assets are we talking about?.

She takes out a folder.

Patrice: All I want is alimony, percentage of the Boutique and the house.

Elliot: Let's check his assets.

Patrice walks over to the window.

Patrice: Nice view up here.

Elliot watches her as she stands in front of the window.

Elliot: Nice view isn't it. (In reference to her)

Patrice: You know Elliot, I won't tell if don't.

She walks over to him and lifts up her dress and straddles his lap.

Patrice: Are we alone?

Elliot: Yes, its only me today; after this I am free and home bound.

Patrice: Good.

He holds her around her small waist line.

Elliot: Patrice are you trying to seduce me?

Patrice: Is it working. I am willing if you are.

Elliot and Patrice go in the back room he takes her silk underwear off and takes his slacks off not to put any wrinkles in it.

They get busy for at least an hour.

Moments later.

Patrice puts on her clothing, shades and grabs her purse.
Patrice: When you figure out how much I'm getting call me.
Elliot sits there in awe. He and Patrice have been best friends for a long time and he never looked at her in a lustful way; up until recently.

One night Patrice was crying on Elliot's shoulder about Mack cheating on her; one thing led to another but they both stopped in the middle for fear it would ruin their friendship.

She goes over to the boutique that she is part owner of.
Mack calls her up.
Mack: Hey baby, I have some free time, I thought we could have lunch.
Patrice: Almost blows her top but she excepts the invitation.
Patrice: Sure. At Al's at 12:05pm.
Mack: See you there.
Mack is trying to be smooth and push what he's doing under the rug.

She continues to the office to look over sales.
Patrice: Della can you come in here for a second.
Della walks in.
Della: Yes.
Patrice: The sales are 1,200 dollars short why?
Della puts her head down.
Della: Well, I hired a new clerk and she was under ringing items to family and friends for about 3 weeks until I found out.
Patrice: I thought we had a security guard.
Della: He was sleeping with her so you know the rest.
Patrice: Order some new gift items and run a just because sale. Let's get some money in here. We have two

clerks that are full-time but we are going to have to cut back. Instead, of giving them 80 hrs. every two weeks we need to cut them down to 60 for at least two month. I suggest you have a staff meeting and as for the the merchandisers, they can stay with the same hours. Once that is done we can talk raise.
Della: Okay.

Patrice makes a call to Elliot.
Elliot: Trice hey!
Patrice: I forgot to mention to you that I have 50% of the boutique, I run it. I want all of it.
Elliot: You know you got that.
Patrice: Oh, what are you doing tomorrow at 9 am.
Elliot: I don't know; you tell me.
Patrice: I'm riding you....if.
Elliot: Where?
Patrice: same time and place as today. (hangs up)
Patrice and Elliot are on there way to a rendezvous. She was once crazy about him until Mack came along and whispered sweet nothings to her and she and Elliot never pursued anything further.

She calls to have her locks changed on the house.
Patrice: Yes, Mr. Fisher, I need to get my locks changed.
    My security code can remain the same. Thanks!
She later goes to see Londa at her office.
Londa: Okay you, what are you up to?
Patrice: Nothing. I am getting what I deserve in my divorce.
Londa: Really. How much in alimony?
Patrice: I figure, with Mack having 5 car dealerships. I should get at least 15 to 20,000 dollars a month.
Londa: How about cleaning him out?
Patrice: No, he needs some cash flow for his tramps.
Londa: Now your being funny.

Patrice: I have a confession. First, I have to call and cancel lunch with Mack. I wanted to break the news to him. But, I am really not up to seeing him.
Londa: What's the confession?
Patrice: Over lunch; please. Let's go to the Sandwich Shoppe.
Londa: I'm ready. Londa has a puzzled look on her face.

Sandwich Shoppe.

Patrice: I got laid today.
Londa: By who?
Patrice: Well, I shouldn't kiss and tell but its been 2 months and I was in the mood.
Londa: Who? Who?
Patrice: Elliot?
Londa: Elliot! My half-brother! And your best friend. But…he's engaged.
Patrice: yes, lower your voice. I just wanted to see what it was like to get laid by that man with smooth silky skin and big feet and hands.
Londa: Okay, you know …he has a woman.
Patrice: I'm not in it for keeps, I just want to get mine.
Londa: okay, but be careful Elliot falls hard.
Patrice: I'm having fun.
Londa: As long as he knows that.
They laugh and talk for a while.
Londa: Don't forget about tonight.
Patrice: I know. I know.
Londa: Are you getting wild on me Ms. "Free Woman"?
Patrice: Not really and don't tell Elliot I told you.
Londa: Girl please. I have to go, I'll see you.

Patrice goes home to relax for awhile. Elliot calls.
Patrice: Hello.
Elliot: Hey, I have it all set. Did you tell him?

Patrice: Not yet. I'm afraid, he won't be happy.
Elliot: I can run the papers to you.
Patrice: Okay, no problem. I'm in the hot tub…

Elliot shows up 30 minutes later.
Patrice opens the door just in her robe.
Patrice: Come in.
Elliot: I can't be around you….because all I want to do is…
Patrice: Is what?
Elliot's cell rings. Turns away to talk.
Elliot: yeah! I'm finishing up for the day. That will be fine.
    I'll be home in about an hour.
Patrice drops her robe. He turns around and things get heated again.
She and Elliot dig into each other.
Patrice: uh….um…ah…..ah.
Elliot is like a machine with high energy.

Evening.

Patrice gets dressed for dinner at Londa's. She brings over desert.
Londa: come in girl. You brought desert; how nice.
Patrice: You got it smelling good girl. I can't wait to try
    some of that scampi.
Londa: John and Calvin haven't made it yet, so I thought
    you could help me with setting the table.
Patrice: I got my papers all set. I shouldn't have waited so
    long to be a free woman. I am going to get over it
    and him.
Londa: It takes some of us longer than others.
Patrice sets the plates down on the table.
Londa: I hope your not planning on going to fast with
    getting involved with someone else so soon.
Patrice: My love for Mack died a long time ago, so If I see
    a good man I will scoop him up.

Londa: I guess that makes sense.
Londa appears worried about Patrice and her sudden moves.

Door bell.
Londa: I'll get it.
John: Hey beautiful.
They kiss
Calvin: Hi Londa, I brought some wine for later.
Londa: Good. Come in.
Calvin looks around.
Londa: She's in the kitchen.
He goes into the kitchen. Patrice is standing at the kitchen cabinet.
Calvin: Hello there.
Patrice: Hey! She walks over to him. I'm sorry about the other day.
Calvin: No….no need to explain. I think I understand.
Patrice: You brought wine.
Calvin: Yes for later.
They find themselves sharing a kiss. Her arms are wrapped around his neck.
Calvin: Tasty.
They break off quickly.

Londa and John joins them.
Londa: Dinner will be ready in about 15 min.
Calvin: Care for that walk now.

Before Dinner.


Calvin and Patrice take a walk.
Calvin: Well, let's start over. I'm Calvin Steele, I am a business owner. I am divorced with a child. I pay alimony. I get visitation with my son Lynel during

the summer and holidays. I have a beach house in Miami and I'm renovating a home here, I have more clientle here so I'm re-locating.
Patrice: Okay. Well, normally I'm a quite person. I am in the middle of a divorce, I am part owner of a boutique and I am hungry.
Calvin: Me too. But first…
He kisses her gently and softly.

Kitchen.

Londa: Dinner is now served.
They all sit and have dinner.
John: Well, Londa I will be traveling again with the team. I have this new client I could make money from.
Londa: I got it Mr. Sport Agent.
John: I want you to come and travel with me next week.
Londa: Woe, I am always supporting your career what about mine.
Patrice: (to Calvin) can you pass me the rolls.
John: Londa baby, I know you're a Law Firm Child Advocate and I want to support your functions and cost and benefits too.
Londa: I'm sorry you guys….
John: Can we talk about it later. (puppy dog look)
Londa: Yeah. I'm sorry. (Changes the subject) How's my cooking?
Calvin: This is good. Its better than my ex-wife.
John: This is better than my sister's cooking for sure.

They laugh.

Patrice: Okay guys, Let's make room for desert.
Later.
They sit and have wine and talk. John and Londa always seem to slip away.

Calvin: John sure loves Londa, she is all he talks about?
Patrice: They been together forever.
Calvin takes her hand.
Calvin: Up for another walk.
Patrice: yeah. You know I thought I'd be married forever but he cheated on me almost throughout our marriage. He had a new woman every 3 months.
Calvin: I know that must be hard.
Patrice: Why did you get divorced?
Calvin: She didn't want to be married anymore. I stayed gone all the time. I wanted a life for us but she didn't see it that way.
Patrice: How long has it been?
Calvin: 2 yrs.
Patrice: I see.
They stop at the end of the sidewalk. He slowly leans in and kisses her lips.
Calvin: I couldn't help it. When I see a beautiful woman like you.
Patrice: I really don't think I am beautiful. Because, I can't understand why a man cheats if he has a good woman who is there for him through thick and thin.
Calvin: A man doesn't have to have a reason.
Patrice: So that's his excuse.
Calvin: I can't speak for all men. I can only speak for myself.

They hear screeching tires from around the corner. Its Mack, he is upset about getting served his divorce papers and the door locks being changed at home.

Patrice and Calvin turn around.
Patrice: Its Mack.
They rush back. He beats on the door of Londa's Condo.
Londa: Mack! What's up?
Mack: Where's Patrice, I know she's here, her car is here.

Londa: She's….
They see her coming down the sidewalk with Calvin.
Mack: (he goes and grabs her by the arm) How could you divorce me after every thing I did for you?
Patrice: Did for me? You never done a damn thing for me!
He slaps her.
Londa lunges to go after him but John buts in.
John: Hey Mack, that isn't cool man hitting on Trice like that.
Macke: You want to make something out of it.
Calvin: Look man, I think you should leave.
Mack: Not without my wife….
Patrice: Let me go. She pulls away.
Mack: Your coming home with me.
Patrice: Why! (yells) After you've screwed all those woman, you expect me to be your wife.
Mack: Okay, I'm wrong okay!…. get in the car and we can drive home and talk about it. Please. (he calms down)
Londa: Trice you don't have to go with him.
Patrice: I know.
Calvin: Are you going to be okay?
Patrice: yeah!
Londa: (to Mack) If you lay one hand on her again you'll regret it.
Mack takes Trice by the hand and they get in the car.

Later.

Londa pacing worried about Patrice.
John: Baby she's going to be okay, I don't think he's crazy enough to do anything crazy.
Calvin left shortly after Patrice went home with Mack.

Mack and Patrice.
Arguing about the divorce.

17

Mack: So its over now!
Patrice: I am not going to repeat myself. I love you too damn much and I get nothing but a man who comes home when he wants too.
Mack: I'll buy you a new house or car. I'll do what I have to, baby give me another chance.
Patrice: At this time, I don't think so. If your not going to leave I will.
Mack: I'm not letting you go so easy.
Patrice: Mack, I don't want you anymore.
Mack: You don't love me.
Patrice: I got enough of this roller coaster. She grabs some clothes and goes to the guest room.
Patrice: you can sleep here tonight but tomorrow, I don't want you here.
She closes the door in his face.
He yells from the opposite side of the door.
Mack: I'm not giving you a divorce. (hit's the door with the side of his fist)

She sits on the chaise in the room and cries. She stays up almost all night. Londa calls to check on her.

Londa: You okay.
Patrice: Yes! I'm good. I can't sleep though.
Londa: You want me to come over.
Patrice: No, stay with John. I'll be fine Londa.
Londa: Well, I'll call you tomorrow.
Patrice goes to take a hot bath. She first makes sure the door is locked before going in.

Early Morning rise.

She gets up from the chaise. She didn't sleep in the bed.
Mack knocks on the door.
Mack: I got breakfast for you baby.

She says nothing and calls Elliot instead.
Elliot is half way asleep.
Elliot: Hello.
Patrice: Hey…starts crying.
He gets up out of bed and goes into the bathroom
Elliot: Trice you okay.
Patrice: No, He's here but I want him evicted from the place. He and I got into a fight.
Elliot: Did he hurt you?
Patrice: No, he grabbed and slapped me and it shucked me up a little but I'm okay.
Elliot: Can you meet me at about 10:00 am and we can go over all of this.
Patrice: Okay.
Elliot: Meet me at the Sandwich Shoppe.
They hang up.
Elliot sneaks into the shower to get dress to meet Patrice.
Elliot is living with his fiancé but he is really starting to get into Patrice again.

She goes into the kitchen.

Mack: I know this breakfast might not change your mind but I want to try.
She stands there for a minute. She goes around him; grabs a cup of coffee walks out of the kitchen.
Mack feels a touch of guilt.

Later.

Londa goes out for breakfast with a co-worker.
Destiny is bragging to a friend about Mack.
Destiny: We will soon be married, I can't wait until he gets rid of that wife of his. She is nothing but a cheater.
Londa listens to Destiny's conversation with her friend.
Destiny: Girl that Mack….

Girl: Mack Allen!…. that rich Entrepunar.
Destiny: Yes. I can't wait.

Londa jumps up from her seat; while still waiting on her co-worker.

She goes to the table where Destiny and her friend are sitting.

Londa: Do you think you're the only woman? You must not know what a liar or cheat Mack Allen really is, he still wants his wife and If I were you I would leave him alone.
Destiny: You can say what you want Missy, I love and want Mack.
Londa: Suit yourself. Your being played.
Destiny turns her nose up at Londa.
Londa decides to leave the shop and meet her co-worker at work. She brings her breakfast at the office instead. She is disgusted with Destiny and her gloating about her and Mack's relationship.

Patrice gets dressed and heads out.
Mack: I'll be home for dinner baby. (he's hoping Patrice will change her mind)
Patrice: You don't get it do you. I want OUT! Besides, you don't have a key to the new locks.
She turns and walks away and grabs a cab to go pick-up her car.

Patrice meets Elliot at the Sandwich Shoppe.
He hugs her.
Patrice: He is unbelievable, he thinks I will work it out this time.
Elliot: I will work on getting him evicted if that's what you want. So, has he been living with you lately.

Patrice: Here. (Hands him a paper) This should help out with who he's been staying with for the past 6 months. All these damn women. A tear rolls down her cheek.
Elliot: Patrice…I will do (he wants to tell her how he feels but says nothing) what I can to help you.
Patrice: You have always been there for me.
Elliot: That's what friends are for.
He takes her by the hand.
She starts to feel a little emotional.
Patrice: I'm sorry. I thought I could hold it together.
Elliot: My shoulder is here and will always.
Patrice: Thanks!

Later.

Patrice goes to the boutique to get her mind off of everything and Calvin walks in.
Patrice: Calvin.
Calvin: Hey. I searched around to find you, so here I am.
Patrice: Come in my office.
Calvin: Are you okay from last night?
Patrice: Yes, I am a fighter.
Calvin: did he hurt you?
Patrice: No. Listen, I'm free for lunch if you want to go for a quick bite.
Calvin: Sure. Oh, maybe I can help your sales with you buying my products for your boutique.
Patrice: Let's see what you have.
Calvin: Stationery, I got from a friend that is selling this design. I am only doing a seasonal run. I'll give you 25 to start.
Patrice: Okay. So lunch?
Calvin: Of course. (he kisses her cheek).
Mack at his car lot. Londa is driving by after seeing a client she stops over to his car lot.

Londa: I'm here to see Mr. Mack Allen.
He comes out of his office with Destiny in his arm. He notices Londa, who is standing there with her arms folded. She shakes her head.

Destiny walks off. She turns to Londa and rolls her eyes.

Londa: You sure know how to work on getting things in order with Trice.
Mack: Trice and I are none of your business. Now, what can I help you with.
Londa: I just came by to confront your trifling tail. How could you be engaged to someone else and still be with Trice. You have real issues.
Mack: You are always fighting Trice's battle's but not today. I'm the man and she is going to take me back. (arrogant)
Londa: Like hell! Not if I have anything to do with it.
Mack: She loves me and she's not going anywhere.
Londa: Don't hold your breathe (she walks out of his office).
Moments Later.

Elliot finishes some paperwork.

He sits there thinking about Patrice. He snaps out of it and realizes he has a girl… Laney.
Laney shows up at his office for lunch.
Laney: Hey baby you ready to go.
Elliot: Yeah! (He closes out his work). They walk out for lunch.

Patrice meets Calvin for lunch.
Calvin: Glad you can make it.
Patrice: If there is one thing I enjoy and that is eating.
They laugh.

Calvin: Order whatever you want.
Patrice: Okay, I want the grilled chicken salad with stuffed shrimps on the side and a Martini.
Calvin: I want a steak well done.
To the waiter.

Calvin: Bring us the bottle of Martini.

Patrice: So, how is your day so far?
Calvin: Better now that I am here with you.
Patrice: Really.
Calvin runs his finger across her nose as a sign of affection. They enjoy lunch.
Calvin: How about coming up to my suite later?
Patrice: Uh….(she notices Elliot with Laney) what time?
Calvin: Whenever your available.
She smiles.

Later.

Patrice goes home to exhale and just before she goes in the hot tub Londa shows up.

Londa: Hey you! (girly hug).
Patrice: You look rushed, what's going on?
Londa: I think you should take Mack to the cleaners.
Patrice: Why?
Londa: He's engaged.
Patrice: What!?
Londa: Yes, I met her today. I confronted him.
Patrice: engaged! (like a ton of bricks just hit her)
Patrice is stunned.
Londa: I thought you should know about this. Don't take him back Trice, he's not worth it.

Patrice sits there frozen.

Mack is in his office at his main dealership and Destiny walks in.

Destiny: Hey lover! She goes over and sits on his lap.

Mack: Hey! Destiny….(he kisses her soft glossy lips).

Destiny: What's wrong?

Mack: I think, Look! I love you, I do but we need to slow it down a bit.

Destiny: Slow it down. She gets up from his lap.

Mack: Yeah! I have a lot to consider in my divorce. (He lies to her) I could lose some of my dealerships. (He was established and has his name and his dad's name are on the dealerships, so Patrice can't take it from him during the divorce procedure).

Destiny: How much time do we have?

Mack: Look, let's just see what happens.

Evening.

Patrice soaks in the tub for at least an hour. She drinks a half a bottle of tequila. She is nearly drunk. She manages to get dressed. She plops on the sofa and flips through the TV station. She looks at the time and looks at the front door. She makes herself some coffee to sober up a little. Calvin waits anxiously for Patrice.

Patrice drinks a few cups of coffee. She realizes her date with Calvin.

She rushes to put on a nice sleeveless causal dress and a nice casual tong slipper with designs. She gets in her car and drives up to his hotel room.

She is a little nervous. She was finally feeling in control of her life and now things are falling a part.

She arrives at Calvin's door a little after 9:00 pm.

Calvin opens the door.

Calvin: I didn't think you were coming.
Patrice: I didn't think I was either.
Calvin: come in.
They share a glass of champagne.
Patrice: Calvin, I shouldn't be here. I am really trying to get over Mack.
Calvin: I didn't think I'd get over my ex-wife until I tried seeing other people.
Patrice: Did it work?
Calvin: Somewhat. I don't want to do anything you don't want to.
Patrice: Right now all I want is....
Calvin: Come here. I know what you need. He pulls her to him and holds her. They put on some soft music and sit in silence.

The next day.

Patrice wakes up by the brightness in the room. She pops up and realizes she was not in her bed.
Calvin walks in with breakfast in bed.
Calvin: Good morning beautiful.
Patrice smiles.
Patrice: You ordered room service.
Calvin: Not exactly. I have a kitchen in here. I went out to the grocery store and got eggs and pancakes, the other stuff is from the hotel.
Patrice: Thank you. Smells good.
He feeds her breakfast in bed.
Patrice: What did we do last night?
Calvin: Well, last night we had a few glasses of wine, we talked, I held you and we both fell asleep. I woke up

and carried you to bed. You still have some things to deal with concerning your soon to be ex-husband…so no we didn't. I would really love to get to know you better. He gives her
Another bite of her pancakes.

Moments past.

Patrice drives home and pulls up in her driveway; only to find Elliot sitting on the front porch with papers in his hand.

Patrice: Elliot!
Elliot: your up early.
He gives her a big hug; as if he missed her.
Patrice feels herself getting horny just being in his arms.
Patrice: Can I invite you in?
Elliot: I….I think I have time.

Elliot and Patrice barely make it to her bedroom. They make love for at least an hour.

Patrice sits up and leans over to Elliot.
Elliot: Yes….(he caresses her face)
Patrice: what is going on between us?
Elliot: I don't know you tell me.
Patrice: Elliot you are a sweet guy and I know your with someone and I'm not trying to get into anything serious and ruin your relationship.
Elliot's heart sinks at the sound but he keeps a manly attitude.
Elliot: your right. I better go.
Patrice: The papers.
Elliot: He has to be out by Thursday, I meet with his attorney today. I'll give you a call.

He walks to the bathroom gets dressed and leaves.

Patrice realizes that she hurt Elliot's feelings. She lays down and pulls the sheets over her head.

Later.

Elliot in his office working on a few divorce cases and Londa shows up.

Elliot: Hey sis!
Londa: Hey! I was in the neighborhood and I decided to stop by and check on my brother. (Looking around his desk suspiciously)
Elliot: I have two nasty divorces to work on.
Londa: Is one Trice's?
Elliot: No, I meet with her attorney today to see what we can settle on.
Londa see's a little disappointment on his face.
Londa: Elliot, did you fraternize with a client?
Elliot: I….
Sec: Mr. Malcolm your fiancé is on the phone.
Elliot: Can you take a message?
Sec: Okay.
Londa: okay brother…..what's going on?
Elliot: Trice, I'm crazy about her.
Londa: No!. You know she's still trying to get over that bastard Mack.
Elliot: Look sis, I am a big boy and I can handle it. I was wrong because I have Laney and we are getting married in a few months.
Londa: yes! So forget about Patrice, I think she just wanted to get laid.
Elliot: Londa, I know….
Londa: Okay, okay. I will say no more. Tonight, John and I are entertaining some of his business tycoon's and I

was wondering if you and Laney can come by tonight.
Elliot: Sure.
Londa: Good, take it easy. (she gives him a peck on his cheek) See you.
He lays back in his chair. With thoughts going through his mind.

John invites Calvin to the dinner.
John: Yeah, bring Trice.
Calvin: What time is the dinner?
John: 7pm.
Calvin: I got your back man.
John: Bring your wallet.
They laugh.

Patrice goes over to the boutique to do some paperwork.
Mack walks in with flowers for Patrice.
Patrice: What in the hell are you doing?
Mack: I was thinking of my wife and wanted to give her flowers.
He brings in a dozen of tulips.
She jerks them from him, goes into her desk draw and cuts the flowers to shreds.
Patrice: I don't want anything but my freedom.
Mack: I made you and I can take you down.
Patrice: Made me.
They get loud and start to argue.
Mack: You are nothing without me.
Patrice: You make me sick.
He grabs her arms.
Patrice: If you don't stop grabbing my arm, I will press charges against you for domestic battery.
Mack: You're my wife. Tonight, I want dinner; in fact I want all of you.

She looks at him for a moment, she almost gets weak and give in to him.
He warms up to her.
Mack: Look, I know I made mistakes but I am willing to change.
Patrice: Oh, Mack please!
Mack: Baby.
He goes around and kiss her on her neck and works his way down her shirt.
Mack: Trice, I am sorry can we work this out.
Patrice turns to him and looks at him.
Patrice: I can't. I won't....its over.
She walks over to the door.
He walks toward the door.
Patrice: By the way, your things will be waiting for you at the door.
Mack: Its not over.
Patrice: Tell that to your fiancé.
She slams the door.

Evening.

Calvin: So you can make it tonight...its to help John and his sports contract.
Patrice: Sure.
Calvin picks Patrice up.
Calvin: Woe, you look lovely.
Patrice: Your looking delicious.
Calvin: Shall we.
They get into his Mercedes. He opens the door to let her in the car and drives away.

Londa's.

Elliot and Laney show up first along with others.

Londa: Hello brother…hey Laney come in.
Calvin and Patrice show up.
Calvin: You will be the most beautiful woman here.
Patrice: Thank you.
They ring the door bell.
Londa: Trice, Calvin..(hugs them).
Patrice and Calvin walk in. John greets them and gets Calvin to mingle with him.
Calvin gives Patrice a peak on the cheek.
Londa: I thought you should know that Elliot and Laney are here.
Patrice: Oh!, ( a little jealous) He and I are just friends.
Londa: yeah (not convinced). Let's have a drink and refreshments.

Patrice mingles a little but not much. Although she is going through her divorce, she still finds herself in a web. She is starting to get attracted to Calvin and she is definitely attracted to Elliot.
Calvin calls for a toast.
Calvin: This is to my long standing buddy John Shaw, this is to his success. He just signed his $5^{th}$ player into the Basketball League. John you're a great man…to his success.

Everyone: Here. Here.

Calvin takes his place next to Patrice. He takes her around her waist.

Elliot looks at them from across the room. He shows signs of jealousy.
Laney: Elliot! You want a drink.
Elliot: I'll get it baby.
Patrice and Calvin hang on to each other most of the night. Patrice somehow breaks away from Calvin. She goes into

the kitchen. The caterer's clean up the kitchen. Patrice stands away from the crowd. She gets away and goes out for air.
Elliot slips by everyone. Laney had to get home she has an emergency at the hospital. Laney is a Doctor.

Patrice sips on her wine and sobs.
Elliot: Nice night isn't.
Patrice: (she continues to look at the stars) It is a nice night…(wipes her face)
Elliot: (doesn't notice she was crying) This is a really nice success for John.
Patrice: He works really heard.
They sit in silence for a little while.
Elliot: I don't know what's going on with me lately… Trice.
Patrice: What do mean? Elliot, You've been there for me so many times, I'm sorry about today.
Elliot: Do you think this is why, I'm…
Londa: There you are. Calvin is looking for you.
Patrice: I better go.
Elliot: Trice we really need to talk.
Patrice: I'll call you.
Londa watches her walk away and looks back at Elliot.

She exits to meet Calvin.

Three weeks has past and Patrice is now divorced from Mack. She had to put a restraining order against him. She is getting 25,000 in alimony, the house and the boutique. She and Calvin has been seeing each other since her divorce. She has not returned any of Elliot's phone calls lately.

In the middle of the day Calvin and Patrice go out for a picnic.

Calvin: I have been enjoying myself just being with you. I will be leaving for Baltimore and I want you to come with me.
Patrice: I don't know. I still have a few things to do.
Calvin: I'll be gone for a couple of weeks. I'm going to miss you.
Patrice: I'll miss you too.
He kisses her neck and makes his way around to her lips. They slowly make love on the blanket at there secluded picnic area near the ocean front.

They make love for the first time. Calvin never pressured Patrice into love making. The ocean water swooshing back and forth while they make music with their bodies.

A few days later.

Londa and Patrice. At Londa's office. They get into a heated conversation.

Londa is upset with Patrice.
Londa: You strung Elliot along just like your doing Calvin. Elliot broke up with Laney because of you, the guilt. You're my friend but you ruin things with Elliot. I know he hasn't told you.
Patrice: Told me what?!
Londa: He's in love with you.
Patrice: I can't do this.
Londa: What do you mean? Your out with Calvin....after you turned Elliot down about a month ago. Trice you're a free woman but you need to get it together.
Patrice: Look who's talking. You're the one who won't support her man in his career. How many times have you flown up to a game and supported John. Don't tell me about Elliot.

Londa: You can take the cheating from a liar like Mack but Elliot's a good and deceit man that you avoiding. What is wrong with you?
Patrice: You can't tell me how to treat a man, when you are having trouble yourself. Whose side are you on anyway?
Londa: I told Elliot he was a fool.
Patrice: I thought I was your friend.
Londa: A friend tells you the truth whether you like it or not!
Patrice storms out of Londa's office.
Patrice (to herself): I see what kind of day I'm going to have.

Elliot's at his place after Laney moved out. He and Laney still talk every now and then.


Patrice goes by his place.

Elliot: Trice! Come in.
Patrice: (Stands there for a while) I'm sorry Elliot, if I gave you misleading....
Elliot: Trice, the first time you and I made love I knew I was missing something. I spent a couple of years with Laney, I learned to love her but I always had a void. He looks her in the eyes. The void.....Patrice is you.
Patrice: Me.
Elliot: For weeks I've had these feelings and they are hard to hide. (paces) Remember the days you came to me crying when you and Mack had a fight. I loved you then. I love you now.
Patrice: You what! Elliot. I'm... no.
Patrice looks at him with a look of confusion.
He takes her in his arms.
Patrice: I really need time.

Elliot: I really need you Patrice. Forget Calvin, what do you know about him.
Patrice: No Elliot. I have to go.
She rushes to the door.
He turns her around and kisses her. He has her up against the doorway. He puts his love inside of her and she gives in.

Moments Past.

Patrice takes a long walk alone.

She sits down on the bench of the lighted park that has secured area near her neighborhood.

She sits and thinks as she listens to the sound of the night.

The next day.

Londa at her office.

Londa toys with whether to call Trice or not. She beats her pencil on her desk.
Flo: She's your best friend. You should call her.
Londa: No. She won't talk to me.
Flo: You never know.
She walks out.

Patrice decides to go for a jog. She returns home after 30 minutes.

She goes in and take a long shower. She pins her hair up and gets in the shower. After her shower, Patrice gets dressed and goes to the Boutique.
Della: We are doing better in sales today.
Patrice: Good. (pre-occupied)

Della: These arrived for you. (dozen of roses)
Patrice: She takes the flowers and smells them.
Della: The card.

Patrice, although you never said you love me or chose to be with me, I love you now and forever. Love, Elliot
Patrice: Della, I'm sorry. I have a decision to make concerning my love life and I've been so occupied with what to do.
Della: I understand....(puts the sales on her desk) She looks back at her. By the way, I have always been told to follow your heart!
Patrice sits and admires her roses for a moment. She toys on her computer trying to decide whether she should call Londa and make up after their fight.

Later.

Patrice goes to the Sandwich shop. Elliot shows up. He orders and goes to sit down and he sees Patrice. His face lights up.
Elliot: Hey beautiful. (his sexy deep voice)
Patrice turns to him. She looks at him. She gets up from the table and plants a big kiss on his lips.
Elliot: what's that for?
Patrice: Can we take this somewhere else?

They head back to her place. They lay down on the great room floor on a leopard skin rug. They wrap up in a silk red blanket and make love until they are sweaty and wet. Moments past, they go in the shower and go for round two. They are dripping wet.

"Kisses" By: Faith Evans--Play in the background.

1 hr. past.

Elliot and Patrice spend the rest of the day laughing and talking.

Elliot: So what does this mean for us? ( he caresses her face)
Patrice: This means I want you….and I love you.
Elliot: I've been waiting to here you say that for a long time now.
They spend time drinking wine and talking.
Elliot: What about Calvin?
Patrice: Elliot, I'm going to handle that. Let's just focus on us.
They spend the rest of the evening together.
Elliot: I'm going to make dinner for us.
Patrice feels happy inside. She just has to find a way to break the news to Calvin.

Calvin finishes his meetings early. He heads back home. He practices over and over in his mind how to ask Patrice to be his wife.

Evening.

Elliot and Patrice spend the evening over a nice candle light dinner.
Patrice: This is delicious.
Elliot: Trice…um I really don't know how to say this but I don't want to lose you.
Patrice: I'm flattered.
Elliot: You deserve the best and I will be that best man for you.
Patrice: I….would like that very much.
They end dinner early and they find themselves back in the sheets.
Next Day.

Londa and John.

John: What's wrong?
Londa: It's Saturday and Patrice and I usually go shopping.
John: And!
Londa: We had a fight.
John: So call her.
Londa picks up the phone and calls Patrice.

Patrice is in the arms of Elliot.
Elliot: Good morning beautiful.
Patrice: Good morning.
Phone rings. She turns over to pick up the phone.
Patrice: Hello.
Londa: Hey!
Patrice: Londa.
Londa: I'm sorry about the other day. I was just angry and I
	don't want you hurt neither do I want Elliot hurt.
	So, can we talk it over say over shopping.
Patrice blushes.
Patrice: Well, (she looks over at Elliot)
Elliot: Go!
Patrice: Okay. Shopping is on.
Later.

Patrice and Londa go shopping.

Londa: So, what's up with you and my brother?
Patrice: We are working on something.
They go into Macy's.
Londa: What about Calvin, who is mad about you?
Patrice: I'm a free woman and I guess I can chose whom I
	want to spend the rest of my life with.
Londa: Woe, did I hear you right.
Patrice: Look at this dress. I want it. I am going to Elliot's

Banquet for his award ceremony. He'll be getting a reward for being Sr. Attorney.
Londa: yeah. He has always been ambitious. How's the Boutique going?
Patrice: I'm making money. Let's go get our feet and nails done.
Londa: Let's go.

They spend a day in the spa. Talking and making up from the fight.

Londa: Your grown and you can make your own decisions.
Patrice just smiles at her.

Calvin is so excited he shows up at Patrice's door soon as his feet hit the ground from his plane ride. He has a 5 carat diamond ring. He rings the doorbell. Elliot opens the door. He is only in his boxing shorts.

Elliot: Can I help you?
Calvin: Yeah..(puzzled) I am looking for Trice.
Elliot: She's out with Londa. Say, you're a friend of John's right.
Calvin: Am, I missing something.
Elliot: I'll let Patrice handle this. You want to come in.
Calvin is puzzled.
Calvin: No, sorry to bother you man.

Calvin walks away with his heart on his shoulder. He drives away and goes over to John's.

John: What's going on man?
Calvin: What's not going on? I can't believe this.
John: What do you mean?
He shows John the 5 carat diamond ring.

Londa and Patrice walk in giggling after having a good time from shopping and girl pampering.

They walk in and see the gloomy look on Calvin's face.
Patrice stops and looks down in shame. She knows what's up?
Patrice: Calvin your back so soon.
Calvin: I had a good reason to come home early until, I
    found out that your seeing someone else.
Patrice: Calvin um…
Londa: Excuse us.
She and John head for the backroom.
Calvin fixes himself a drink.
Calvin: I thought, I knew what I wanted. I thought you
    knew what you wanted.
Patrice says nothing. She looks on the table and sees the ring box.
Calvin: I really thought you and I would become one.
Patrice's heart drops.
Patrice: Calvin, I am really sorry.
Calvin: When were you going to tell me?
Calvin is crushed.
Calvin: You called me all day everyday that I was
    away….you lied every time we hung up. I thought
    you of all people would be different.
Patrice: I am sorry Calvin. I didn't mean for this to be like
    this. I care about you but….
Calvin: I understand Trice. You've been hurt so much your
    confused and I was wrong. I'm okay with this.
He pulls himself together.
Patrice: Sometimes, when you feel something is right you
    just go for it. I had no idea that it would be like this.
    Yes, my intentions were to be with you, love you
    and all that but I feel something more for Elliot.
Calvin tucks in his bottom lip.
Calvin: I guess it just wasn't meant to be that's all.

He gives her a long hug. Tears roll down her face.
He pulls away from her slowly and walks to the front door.
Calvin: I'm here if you need a friend.
Patrice: Don't you want to give this to a special person.
   Hands him the box.
He opens the door and walks out.

George Michael "Never gonna dance again"---
Calvin takes a long drive. He thinks about all his time with Patrice. He drops by a 24 hr. Wedding Chapel. He talks to a couple and hands the man the ring box. He drives off into the sunset with thoughts of Patrice.

Londa joins Trice.

Londa: you okay.
Trice shakes her head.
Londa: Move forward. You have a man at home waiting on you.
Londa: I know you feel bad about Calvin but sometimes things in life are uncomfortable. Don't stay with Calvin and wonder what it would be like to be with Elliot. But when your with Elliot make the best of your life. You've been through too much. Now, Go!
Patrice smiles with confidence.


Evening.

Patrice and Elliot get ready for the Banquet.

Elliot: You look gorgeous.
Brian McKnight plays softly in the background. "Anytime"
Patrice: Do you hear the music?
Elliot: Yes.

They dance slowly in each other's arms.

The moments from the past plays of the time Patrice and Elliot were only friends and almost lovers. They went to games together, shopping, movies, swimming and the dreadful night she got into a fight with Mack. He saved her life by allowing her to stay the night with him.

Patrice and Elliot head out to the Banquet.

Elliot: Forever, My Free Woman!
They drive off to the Banquet holding hands and every now and then they look at each other and blow each other a kiss.

Shortly, after a short engagement Elliot and Patrice got married. She is expecting with twins. They move into Elliot's house. Elliot finally has his own Firm with two other Attorney's working with him. Londa and John got married, she now travels with him. She doesn't have to work, so she only works part-time. Mack and Destiny never got married. They are still engaged because he still wants to be with Patrice. He stays away from Destiny by booking out of town meetings because Destiny is a nagging woman and he finds excuses to stay away from her.

Meanwhile, Calvin Steele continues to have a successful business. He dates occasionally but he vowed never to give his heart to another for a long time. He and Patrice are friends.

Patrice at home alone making dinner for her and Elliot.

She calls Calvin.
Calvin: How's it going?

Patrice: Good. I have three more months before the babies come.
Calvin: You deserve to be happy. I'll never forget you.
Patrice: Thank you and neither will I.
They hang up in silence.

# Weary and Tare

Desiree Keel  
Earl Bates  
Tyresha Kindle  

Bill Payton  
Violet Stern  
Lollie Davis  

Tyresha and Bill are at it again. He is still not bringing the money home legally.
Bill rushes home to freshen up and the whole time Tyresha is getting on his case about him not being home.

Tyresha: Bill, I've been calling you for hours, where in the hell have you been?
Bill: Don't question me woman.
Tyresha: I can't keep sitting here all day waiting on you

and you don't show up. My parents are coming to meet you.

Bill: I have something to do, I won't be here.

Tyresha: Woe! You promised.

Bill: I have to make a hustle, if you want to keep your self-groomed, I need to make some money.

Tyresha: Okay fine! Go! (shows him the door)

He walks out.

Tyresha: (to herself) I don't need him. I have a college degree and I am stuck in this small ass apartment with nothing but bills…(she goes through the mail).

She sees a strange envelope. She hesitates to open it. She rushes to her desk drawer to get her letter opener.

She opens the letter and a check falls out. A letter from her parents telling her they can't make it but this check should cover expenses for the month.

Tyresha glances at the check.

Tyresha: A check for 10,000. She starts jumping up and down (excited).Okay, okay. She goes in the shower to ready get to go out with her friends Desiree and Lollie.

Desiree and Lollie just got out of the hair salon and walk over to Tyresha's apartment.

Desiree: This girl really needs to get rid of that loser Bill. He is wearing her down.

Lollie: I know, she needs to get with somebody like my brother Mitch.

Desiree: Mitch! He is a successful business man, he doesn't want anybody like Tyresha.

Lollie: Tyresha is a deciet girl and friend. Your mad because he doesn't want you; trick!

Desiree: He is fine. Maybe, I am a little loose with it and he didn't want none of me because he was scared.

Lollie: Whatever, let's get up there and see if she's ready.

Desiree: I wonder what's the good news.
They knock on the door to Tyresha's apartment. Her parents have been paying her bills since she left home.

Tyresha: Coming. She opens the door.
Lollie: Hey girl!
Desiree: Hey you ready. I am ready to meet somebody.
Tyresha: Do you like this? Shows them a pair of hip hugger jeans with a silky black low cut shirt and black heels to match. Her hair is spiked up with honey blonde tips.
Desiree: That looks good but not as good as me.
Desiree has always been arrogant and conceited. She thinks too highly of herself. No one ever looks as good as her.
Lollie: It looks good girl! Let's go.
Desiree: First the good news!
Tyresha: Look at this. She shows them the check.
Desiree: Give me some.
Lollie is the level headed one next to Tyresha. Tyresha is intelligent but she seems to have a weakness for Bill, who does nothing for her.
Lollie: You need to pay your bills and save…save…save.
And don't tell Bill because then your money is well spent.
Tyresha: yeah! I will deposit it first thing tomorrow.
She runs and hides it in her safe on her side of the closet and hides the key.
She gives herself one last look in the mirror and they go out for a girls night out.

Club Ion.

Club Ion is upscale for casual drinkers and college students and lonely businessmen.

They find a nice quite table. A nice fine waiter with only a bow tie around his neck and slacks come to there table.
Waiter: May I help you?
Desiree: yes, your phone number would be nice…but tonight give us all a margarita.
Desiree reaches over and pats the waiter on the butt.
Lollie: Your going to get us thrown out of here (between her teeth).
Tyresha sits down so studios and upright that she catches the eye of a nice handsome stockbroker named Earl Bates. Earl is five foot eleven inches tall with a caramel color with nice curly hair.
Tyresha notices him looking at her, he raises his glass to her to acknowledge he sees her.
She squirms a little.
Waiter: Ladies your drinks. Oh, by the way, drinks are on the house from the gentleman at that table. It was Earl Bates.
Desiree: You know him (to Lollie) and you Tyresha, you might want to get some night.
Tyresha: Why do you say that, I'm not the one who gets laid every chance she gets.
Desiree: See you!
They laugh.
Sip on their drinks.
Desiree: I am going to find the father of my baby tonight. Watch me.
Tyresha: Whatever, what about last week, that guy Preston. He was all over you until you saw he had a missing tooth.
Lollie: Oh yeah! What about Justin…Justin Curtsy, He was so fine until you got him back to your place Desi and he wasn't as fine when you found out his underwear had a hole in it.
Tyresha: Okay, I'm sorry. No more funny stories, he's coming over.

Desiree: I bet you $20 he's coming to talk to me.
Lollie: I bet $40 he wants Tyresha.
Desiree: Okay, winner takes all.
Earl approaches.
Earl: Hello ladies, I hope you didn't mind me buying you all a drink.
Desiree: Not at all. (licking her lips)
Earl: So, (looking at Tyresha) what may I ask is your name?
Tyresha: Tyresha Kindle, this is my friend Lollie and Desiree.
Earl: Well, Tyresha do you mind coming out on the terrace with me.
Tyresha: (looks at her friends and smiles) Sure. He takes her hand and they go out for air.
Lollie: Winner takes all. (hand out for her cash)
Desiree: What about? (snaps her fingers) Leroy; remember him. I wonder if he is here tonight.
Lollie: Who knows!
Desiree: I am going to take a stroll and see what I can sniff out.
Lollie sits alone until a bi-racial hunk walks by.
Man: Hello. Sitting alone.
Lollie: Yes, You want to sit.
Man: Sure. Hi, I'm Pierce.
Lollie: Lollie as in Lollie Pop.
They laugh.
Pierce: Can I get you another (drink)?.
Lollie: I didn't realize it was gone.
They re-order drinks.

Meanwhile, Tyresha is out on the Terrace with Earl.
Earl: So do you come here often?
Tyresha: Twice a week.
Earl: I just started coming here. I just moved here from Florida. I was hoping to run into a fine…I mean a nice woman like you.

Tyresha: (blushes) I….so why did you move here.
Earl: Business. I am a Stock Broker. I'm following the money.
Tyresha: I just graduated from College 6 mo. Ago. My parents pay my bills. I…have two crazy friends.
Earl: Yeah. Listen, how about having lunch with me tomorrow.
He goes in a little closer. Almost touching her lips.
Tyresha: I….well, I don't have a car. I totaled it and never got a replacement yet.
Earl: How about I pick you up? Here's my card.
He gives it too her but holds it tight. She tries pulling the card away from him.
Earl: How about another drink?
Tyresha: Okay.
He admires her smooth face and her nice figure. They resume at the table. Lollie is cuddled up with Pierce trying to get to know him. Lollie is single and loves it. She lives in a Loft a few blocks down.
Desiree got a few numbers but she is not taking anyone home tonight because Ed is waiting back home for her. Ed is a long time friend, who comes by every now and then. They enjoy pleasing each other.

Evening is over.
Tyresha gets a ride home with Earl. Lollie takes a cab home escorted by Pierce. Desiree stays at Club Ion because she ran into an old friend named William. She later goes back to his place until Ed blows up her cell phone.

Tyresha and Earl.
Tyresha: Thanks. Can you drop me off right here?
Bill is outside with some of his friends.
Tyresha: thanks…
Earl: Should I get out and walk you to the door.

Tyresha: No…no (sees Bill). I'll call you. She slips his
    number in her undies (back of jeans).
Bill sees her from a distance walking down the sidewalk.
Bill: Where have you been?
Tyresha: Out with Desiree and Lollie.
He looks down the sidewalk sees a cab drive off.
Bill: you sure your not screwing around on me.
Tyresha: I'm tired, I don't have time for this Bill…really.
Bill: See you man (some of his loser buddies).
Says bye to his friends.
They go upstairs.
She goes to the bedroom. Bill follows.
Bill: I've been missing you. I want a piece of my woman.
    He kisses her as if he can't get enough. They get
    undressed. He takes her to ecstasy. They get under
    the sheets for at least an hour.

Later.

She and Bill lie down by candle light.
Bill: I am working on getting a legal job. I take it your
    parents didn't come.
Tyresha: No, that's why I went out with the girls.
Bill: You know I love you right.
Tyresha: Yeah, I know. She turns away and he cradles next
    to her.
Bill: We made love and it was good but are you still mad
    about Violet.
Tyresha: You apologized about Violet ten times. I am over
    it. (sound of frustration in her voice)
Bill: I just wanted to know where we stood baby. He kisses
    her on her back and goes to sleep.
She rolls her eyes. Tyresha is not over Bill's cheating.

Next Day.

Desiree jumps out of bed and heads to work. She works as a Wedding Consultant. She showers and puts on a sun dress. Ed lays there as she gets ready for work.

Desiree: Shouldn't you be getting ready for work.
Ed: I work for my dad, I'm never on time.
Desiree: Anyway, Are you making dinner today?
Ed: I can dear.
Desiree: I have 4 appt. at $300 each, I've made my quota
       for the day.
Ed: ( he slaps her backside)
Desiree: I don't have time this morning.
She rushes out. He lays back down.

Tyresha goes to the bank before Bill wakes up.
She puts 5,000 in one account and 3,000 in another and takes 2,000 to pay her bills and get groceries.
She stays out awhile shopping. She sits in the café staring at Earl's card. She toys with her cell phone wondering if she should call him or not. She looks at the time and then back at her phone. She decides to make the call.

Tyresha: Yes, Earl Bates please. Um…Tyresha Kindle yes
       an investment. (to herself) On him of course.
Earl: Hello angel.
Tyresha: Hi! I was wondering if you were available for
       lunch?
Earl: Yes, meet me 600 NE Laney or should I pick you up.
Tyresha: No, I have a way.
Tyresha goes over to Lollie's.

Lollie's. Tyresha knocks on her door.
Lollie: (just awakening) Pierce in the shower.
Tyresha: I am with you all day, if Bill asks. I'm going to

have lunch with Earl. Um, Is your car still in the shop.
Lollie hands her the keys.
Tyresha: Thanks! (hugs her and rushes off)
Lollie rubs her face. She realizes that Pierce is still there. She joins him in the shower.

Tyresha arrives at the address 30 minutes later.
Tyresha parks Lollie's BMW and walks in the restaurant.
Hostess: Can I help you?
Tyresha: I'm having lunch with Earl Bates.
Hostess: Right this way.
He leads her to Earl's table. It is a closed in private booth. It is glass proof that drowns out the noise.
Tyresha: This is a nice place.
Earl: I thought you would like it.
Tyresha tries to relax.
Earl: I didn't think you were coming.
Tyresha: I did give it a lot of thought.
Earl: Well, you can have whatever you want.
Tyresha loved the way those words rolled off of his lips so freely.
Earl: I had a good time last night.
Tyresha: So did I.
Earl: If you don't mind me asking, how is your apartment? I mean do you like it.
Tyresha: It is a small apartment, its all I can afford right now. My parents help out.
Earl: I see. So what did you get a degree in?
Tyresha: Business Management. I was teaching during the summer at the Jr. college but I had to take some time off.
Earl: Are you looking for work?
Tyresha: yes and no. I….why?
Earl: I could use some help in my Broker business. I have a Seminar coming up and I need some help.

Tyresha: I don't know.
Earl: It pays 45.00 an hour. With benefits.
Tyresha: I'll think about it. I'll have a grilled shrimp salad.
Earl: You don't eat much do you, no wonder your so um….
Tyresha: I really don't eat much.
Earl: You have such a beautiful smile.
Tyresha's face lightens up at his comment.
They order and eat lunch.

Bill meets up with some friends to make a hustle.
Bill: Look Dek, I am not doing this anymore. I need to work legally before I lose my woman.
Dek: Who Violet? Everybody knows your still seeing her.
Bill: Look, I have to take care of my unborn child.
Dek: She's pregnant for you man…..oh no. What about Tyresha?
Bill: I love her and she knows it.
Dek: yeah but one night with Violet is costing you all that booty.
Bill: Well, look let's make this hustle and get out of here.

Desiree finishes up with her clients. She goes shopping and runs into Lollie.
Desiree: Do you think Tyresha hit it off with that guy last night?
Lollie: Maybe!
Desiree: Hey, I am not going to hate on her or anything.
Lollie: My point exactly.

Earl and Tyresha finish lunch.
Tyresha: I had a great time, I really have to get going.
Earl: What about the Seminar?
Tyresha: I'll call you.
She makes her way out the door. He tramples behind. He walks her to the car.

Earl: If you don't mind. He goes in for a kiss. She turns her face and he gives her a peck on the cheek.
Then she gets in the car and drives off.

She returns to her apartment. Bill is at home waiting on her to arrive.
Bill: Hey baby, where you been?
Tyresha: Filling out job applications.
Bill: You usually do that on the computer.
Tyresha: Well, the one's I filled out I had to do in person. (sharp tone)
Bill: I thought maybe we could hang out tonight. Have a barbeque and invite a few friends over.
Tyresha: Okay. (thinking of Earl)
Bill: I'll prep the grill.
Tyresha: I'll see if Lollie and Desiree will come over with some friends.
He goes on the balcony. She turns and goes in the bedroom. She freshens up, because she has to bring Lollie her car back. She slips past Bill.
Dek is outside the apartment.
Dek: Well…well, how's it going?
Tyresha: Good Dek, how's Tonya?
Dek: Finer than ever.
Tyresha: Well, Bill wants to have a barbeque tonight, so will you come….bring Tonya.
Dek looks at her as if he feels she knows what's up with Bill and Violet.
Dek: yeah, we'll be there.

Tyresha decides to go to Earl's office before bringing Lollie her car back.
Lady: Tyresha Kindle is here.
Earl: Please send her in.
Tyresha: Wow! This is nice. (In reference to his office. Earl has a glass executive desk with a brown leather

chair with a flat screen computer; with a nice window view)
Earl: I love to attract people. Come let me show you the view.
She stands looking out the window and he goes behind her. Their body heat gets a little intense.
Tyresha: Beautiful view. She nearly melts feeling him this close to her.
Earl: So, what brings you by?
She turns to him.
Tyresha: The job offer.
Earl: That's all.
Tyresha: Yes, where do I begin?
They have a seat.
Earl: Here's the paperwork. He touches her hand during the paperwork exchange.
Tyresha: I will um….bring it back tomorrow.
Earl: I can't wait.
Tyresha: I'll call if I have questions. (reviewing the application and requirements)
She gets up and walks out but looks back at him, whose looking right at her. They exchange smiles.

Later.
Barbeque.
Lollie and Tyresha near the kitchen area.
Lollie: you know roamer has it that Bill is still seeing Violet.
Tyresha: That's what I didn't want to believe.
Lollie: Why are you wasting your time with him anyway. He is not doing anything for you. He doesn't work, he doesn't own a car or his own place.
Tyresha: Yeah, I know but….Bill and I are working through all of this.
Lollie: Okay, but I warned you. He is a (L sign with her hand) loser.

Desiree walks in with Ed.
Tyresha: Hello you two. Ed hasn't been around in awhile.
Desiree: Okay Esha don't go snooping around my man like you did the last one.
Tyresha: Desi please!
They laugh.
Bill goes over to Tyresha and gives her a kiss on the neck.
He grabs her around her waste.
Lollie looks at them like this is a waste.
Lollie nibbles on snacks while waiting on Pierce to show up.
Tyresha gets away from Bill.
Tyresha: So, where is Pierce? I know you scored with him.
Lollie: yes, he is great!
Tyresha: you say that about all the men you sleep with.
Lollie: He is real, he is not a irresponsible nerd.
Tyresha: Well, I've been thinking a lot about Earl. I am even thinking about giving him something to call my name.
Lollie: How can you do that, when you have Bill sniffing around.
Tyresha: I never told Earl that, I was seeing anyone. Well, he's never asked.
Lollie: Well, take it slow.
They stand and talk with their lips barely showing movement and smiling occasionally because Bill is always so suspicious of her.
Tyresha: Well, I better mingle with the others.
She takes a walk toward the balcony and she hears Bill on the phone. Dek steps away to get some more to drink.
Bill: Look, I am here with my girl having a little get together. I can't please….(pleading his case) you and her.
Tyresha clears her throat.
Bill hangs up the phone.
Tyresha: Smells good out here.

Bill: Thanks! Dek man can you watch this, I have to run out right quick. Can I get your keys?
Tyresha: Where are you going?
Bill: We are running low on some refreshments.
Tyresha: I can get that for you.
Bill: I got it baby. Keep the party going.

Bill rushes off. He picks up refreshments but ends up at Violet's.
Violet: Glad you can make it.
Bill: I don't have much time.
Violet: I just needed to see you.
They spend a few moments kissing.
Bill: we'll finish this later.
Violet: promise.
Bill: Yes!
Kisses her by and rushes off.

The party is going on. Dek finishes up the barbeque.
They have fun, dance and slow dance like the school days.

Moments Past.

Lollie waits for Pierce. He arrives really late.
She puts on a big cheesy smile. She thrust her body to the door.
Lollie: I've been waiting for you.
Pierce: I got tied up. I went out of town on a few business deals and traffic held me up. I wanted to be here. I promised.
Pierce: Since, I'm late can we go somewhere private.
Lollie: Okay.
They slip away from the party.
Pierce: Here you go. (plants a kiss on her lips)
Desiree and Ed are all over each other.

Dek is with Tonya. Others mingle and make out and some are eating.

Moments Past and the party is over.
Tyresha sees everyone out. Bill slipped by her during the time the others left.
This time she doesn't care, she found a man….a real man.
She starts cleaning up the apartment. She starts to think about her life and about what Lollie said about Bill being a loser.

Bill is with Violet. Things are hot and heavy between the two of them. They both pant for air.
Violet: I couldn't wait for this. (panting for air)
Bill thrusts her again.

Meanwhile, Lollie and Pierce go back to her place. They have martini's and wine. They both get tipsy. Before the night is over, Lollie finds herself on his lap. They begin to kiss each other passionately.

Lollie: I'm not one for words. They kiss each other until,
       she leads him to her bedroom. She kicks her shoes
       off at the end of the hallway.
Music by Brian McKnight plays softly.

Tyresha cleans up the mess and goes for a shower. She stays in the shower for at least 30 minutes. She gets out dries herself off and puts on her bathrobe. She sits down on the sofa looking over her job opportunity. She flips through the pages. She gets a pen and starts to fill in the blanks.

Next Day.

Every Saturday Tyresha makes breakfast for her and Bill but the only problem is that he is not home. She gets dressed and heads out to go car shopping. She rushes out and catches a cab. She ends up at an Infiniti and Jaguar Dealership. She steps out the cab. Behind the cab is a BMW. Earl was on his way to see her but decides to follow her instead.

She gets out and starts looking around. Earl walks in the dealership snatches a sales person and tells him to give her any car she wants. Earl sits in the lobby in the meantime. The sales person joins Tyresha.
Tyresha: Tyresha Kindle (Shakes his hand).
Sales person: Hi! I'm Joey Patrick. I'll be your sales person today. What can I help you with?
Tyresha: I am loving this Jaguar and this Infiniti.
Joey Patrick: What If I tell you that whatever car you want you can have?
Tyresha puzzled.
Joey: Yes! So, how about this Jaguar?
Tyresha: I don't know. What's the down payment?
Joey: For you nothing.
Tyresha: Okay, (gets ghetto with it) if its booty you want, its booty your not going to get.
Joey: No, Come let me explain the special we are having today.
They walk into the dealership and straight into Joey's office.
Joey: Have a sit. I'll be right back.

Joey goes over to talk to Earl.
Joey: She loves the Jaguar.
Earl: Here's the check.
Joey: What do I tell her?
Earl: Fix the paperwork, give her the keys and I'll handle the rest.

Bill and Violet.

Bill: I have to go.
Violet: When will you be back lover?
Bill: Soon. I'll call you.
He gives her a kiss good bye.

He goes home only to find Tyresha gone.

He sees her application on the table and thinks about getting a honest job.

He goes different places to get applications, Now hiring signs. Some people turned him down and others said they are not hiring right now. He gets upset and calls up Dek.

Bill: Hey Dek, got a gig?
Dek: I thought you were out.
Bill: Naw, I need some fast money. Trying to please two women is not easy.
Dek: You got problems. Meet me on $27^{th}$ and $3^{rd}$ in an hour.
Bill: Cool.

Car Dealership.
Joey finalized the paperwork.
Joey: Sign here and here. Handing her the pen to sign.
Tyresha: So the Jaguar is really mine.
Joey: yes.
She signs the papers, he hands over her copies and the keys.

She rushes outside only to find Mr. Sexy leaning against her car.
The Jaguar is of a plum color with peanut butter leather seats and a moon roof.
Earl: Like your new car.

Tyresha: Wait....I got this car for nothing....and you're here. How did you know, I was here?
Earl: I was on my way to see you and I saw you drive off, so I followed you. Besides, if anyone is going to work for me, she is going to drive the best.
Tyresha: I don't want to get this all twisted now Earl.
Earl: you won't. Look, you are a beautiful woman with brains and someone who I want to give a try at my Broker business. Do you have your application filled out?
Tyresha: I do. I will have to stop by my apartment and pick it up, but not until I show my ride to my girls.
Earl: I'll see you.... say in an hour.
Tyresh: Okay.
Earl: Congratulations on your car.

They go separate ways.
Tyresha is so excited she goes by Lollie's first.
She beats on the door like the police.
Lollie: What's up?
Tyresha: Come see my car.....she pulls her downstairs.
Lollie: Woe! This is fine. This is better than my Beemer.
Tyresha: Yes. Guess what?
Lollie: What's the story?
Tyresha: My new boss wanted to see me in style.
Lollie: So, Earl bought you this.
Tyresha: I um...I went to look and the sales person came to me and sold it to me with no money down.
Lollie: He paid for this cash. Girl, you better grab him girl. I'm going upstairs and grab by purse, let's go for a spin.
They drive over to Desiree's.
Desiree and her smart mouth.
Desiree: Okay, Who did you give up the booty too?
Tyresha: Very funny Missy. For your information it comes with my new job. My boss wants me in style.

Lollie: Okay…girls lets go for that ride.

Bill makes a few exchanges. He goes home and counts out the money.
Bill: 2,000. I'll give $800 to Tyresha and $500 for Violet.
He waits awhile and then goes over to Violet's.

Bates Brokerage Inc.
Tyresha drives up in her new car. She is dressed in a ivory pant suit with silver pumps accenting her pedicure. She walks in the building with confidence and a steaming hot cup of mocha. She walks up to Earl's receptionist.
Betty: You must be Tyresha Kindle. Earl is waiting for you. Go in.
She takes a deep breath then walks in his office.
Earl: Hello. (standing near the window)
Tyresha: Hi!
Earl: I have your office all set. Come let me show you.
Her office is right across from his.
Her office is nicely wall papered with sage green trimmings. A glass desk with a flat plasma computer. A built in book-self and her own private bathroom. She has two chairs, if she has company over to her office.
Earl: First, I want to show you the program.
Earl goes on to show her the place, the program and the mission of the company. He gives her accounts to work on. He departs for a meeting.
Tyresha relaxes in her new office. She rares back in class.

Desiree and Lollie go shopping.
Lollie: Let's get Tyresha something for her office.
Desiree: She has a car, what more can she want!
Lollie: She is our best friend in case you forgot.
They walk past Macy's and see Bill with Violet.
Desiree nudges Lollie.
Desiree: See why I don't blame her for taking that car.

They see Bill and Violet hugged up.
Lollie: I can punch him in his mouth.
Desiree: How about the groin?
Lollie: Take it easy tiger!!!!

Bill and Violet go into Children's World. Violet steps out from behind the rack and they see her protruding stomach.

Lollie: What the hell? Let me at him ….(She makes a charge and Desiree pulls her back).
Desiree: I got a better idea. (She takes a picture with her cell phone).
Lollie: Let's get out of here.

Tyresha is invited to lunch by Earl.
He takes her to a quite place. They sit at a table way in the back of the Restaurant.
Earl: How's your first half day?
Tyresha: Relaxing.
Earl: I have a meeting at 3pm, you think you can join me.
Tyresha: Sure. Unless, my boss has another assignment for me.
Earl: I don't think so.
Tyresha: Thanks again for the car.
Earl: So tell me, are you seeing anyone? I forgot to ask. I'm sure you know….that…
Tyresha: I am seeing someone but we are so different.
Earl is disappointed but tries not to show it.
Earl: A beautiful woman like you should have a man in her arm.
Tyresha: (blushes) I….what about you, are you dating anyone?
Takes a sip of her drink.
Earl: Not at the moment but I would like to start seeing this beautiful woman I just met. He leans forward and gives her a kiss on her soft glossy lips.

Tyresha lets out a moan.
Earl: Ready to order.
Tyresha: Um…only if your ready.
He goes in for another kiss. They slowly kiss intimately. His kiss is like mom's apple pie with whip cream and cherries. His kiss is delicious.
Earl: Come see me tonight.
Tyresha: I….(she can barely resist) let me think about it.
He looks at her and smiles.
Earl: I like how you are so careful.
Earl and Tyresha return to work from brunch laughing and having a good time. Every now and then his arms slips around her waste.

Desiree and Lollie look over at them with delight.
Desiree: Well…..Well, we came by to bring you a gift and your out having too much fun.
Lollie: She's the most outspoken person I ever met. Anyway, hello Earl.
Earl: Hello Lollie and you must be Desiree.
Tyresha: yeah, that would be Desi.
Lollie: We bought something for your office.
Earl: Excuse me ladies, oh Tyresha meeting at 3pm.
Tyresha: Okay.
They go to her office.
Desiree: This is one bad office.
Tyresha: Thank you…
Lollie: Oh, here you go a nice plant for your office.
Tyresha: Thank you guys. She puts it on the shelf.
Lollie: We have something to tell you.
Tyresha: If its about Bill, I don't want to hear it.
Desiree and Lollie look at each other.
Lollie: He's still seeing Violet.
Tyresha: I don't believe that. (playing with her plant)
Desiree: Maybe, I should show her.
Desiree walks over to her and shows her the picture.

Tyresha: This doesn't mean anything.
Lollie: What is wrong with your vision?
Desiree: You better open up your eyes, you just got this fine office with this fine job, a fine car and maybe a fine man to go with it.
Tyresha let's that last comment sink in. She turns to her friends.
Tyresha: I love the plant.
They look at her dumbfounded. Its as if she didn't hear them.
Desi: Bill's a loser and you still want him.
Tyresha: He was there for me when I was in college, he understood me when you two didn't….! Don't you remember. (upset)
Desi: Okay, he's going to break your heart. Look at what you have here.
Lollie: You are going somewhere in your life and Bill, he's still selling drugs on the streets. What kind of life is that? You two are like night and day.
Tyresha: I don't want to hear anymore.
Lollie: Okay! Can we count on you to meet us at Club Ion?
Tyresha gives a slight smirk.
Desi: Club Ion is going to be booming with the sexiest men alive.
Lollie: Cool your heels girl, Ed is marked in and engraved on that!
Tyresha: I'm sorry girls, I will pick you up in my new car.
They hug each other and leaves her office.
Tyresha slumps in her chair.

Earl knocks on the door.
Tyresha sits up.
Tyresha: Come in.
Earl: 15 mintues before the meeting, you ready to walk down.
Tyresha: Sure. She grabs a legal tablet and a pen.

They walk to the small conference room and meet up with a few other people. It is a small privately own corporation.

Earl: Let's get started. Everyone this is Tyresha Kindle our new addition.
Voice fades out as he conducts the meeting.

Moments Past.

Earl and Tyresha part for the evening.
Earl: My offer is still open, if you change your mind.
Tyresha: Okay. Thanks again.

She drives home to her hood apartment. She drives past the place and goes to get a newspaper to do apartment shopping.
Tyresha: (to herself) It's time to move on. I want to move on but without Bill. He's caused me pain with being with Violet and if she is really having his baby, he doesn't need me. I have a rich and fine man who wants me. I think I want him but what do I do. Bill is so good to me intimately, what if Earl is not all that. At least he's rich. Okay, I'm getting a new place. How do I explain the car to Bill?.

She walks in the apartment. The apartment is clean with a fresh pine scent. She sees $800 dollars on the table. She picks it up and puts it back down.

She then goes into her closet to pick out something to wear for Club Ion.

Desiree and Lollie. Lollie's Loft.

Desiree: Do you think she heard us today? I mean, Bill is

fine and all and when he makes his hustle he does break her off some.

Lollie: So, What does that mean? He needs an honest job. I know she might love him but she is moving up in her life.

Desiree: So, now that she is on her feet, after he stood by her, she has to leave him…

Lollie: No, Look, If a guy sees a woman doing something positive he should want the same.

She grabs a soda out of the Fridge. Gives Desiree a drink.

Lollie: I want her to have the best. She is like a sister to both of us right….(looking at Desiree)

Desiree pretends not to hear her.

Desiree: (laughs) yes girl!

Lollie: Club Ion is on tonight, I better check on Pierce, I wonder if he's going to join me.

Desiree: Thanks for the coke but I have to get going. I have to please Ed before going out or I'm doomed.

Lollie waves her bye.

Tyresha pulls out a short red dress with a zagged look. She then pulls out the red pumps. She thinks about asking Earl to join them.

She hears the sound of the keys in the door.

Bill: Hey baby! I'm home.

Tyresha: In here. She doesn't feel like being bothered but plays along.

He goes in the room and puts his arms around her. He kisses her on the neck.

Bill: (whispers) I love you. Did you get the money I left you?

Tyresha: Yeah. Thanks!

He sees her dress on the bed.

Bill: Where are you going?

Tyresha : Out with the girls.

Bill: I thought maybe you and I could spend tonight together.
Tyresha: We can...but. You know me and the girls....we
Bill: I'll go with you.
Tyresha: What!
Bill: I'm going with you. By the way, Why is that Jaguar parked in our apartment spot?
Tyresha: I bought it today.
Bill: You what! Where did you get the money?
Tyresha: I, my credit was so good I didn't need any money down.
Bill: Oh, really, Its nice. I guess we will be going to Club Ion in style.
She smiles nervously.

Later at Club Ion.

Tyresha and Bill arrive first, so they reserve a table.
Lollie walks in with Pierce in her arms bobbing her head.
Desiree is on the prowl again and takes a walk around first.
Tyresha walks them down.
Lollie: Hey you two, the place is bumping tonight.
Tyresha: Yes! It is.
Lollie plays this off by telling Tyresha she has lipstick on her teeth.
Lollie: To the girls room...Esha.
They go to the girls room.
Lollie: Okay, what's up with you bringing Bill.
Tyresha: He is still my boyfriend.
Lollie: What if Earl shows up?
Tyresha: I doubt it. I really didn't want him to come but...
Lollie: Okay, play it cool, you look good.

They walk out to go back at there table. The first person standing at the door is Earl. He is standing there with a woman with a light caramel complexion with a open back sky blue dress. She sees him but tries to walk past him. He walks over to her.

She and Lollie stop in the middle of the floor.

Earl: Tyresha, I'd like you to meet Lynda……. my sister. She's visiting me from out of town. This is her friend Lollie.

Tyresha: Nice to meet you. (She catches her breath)

Earl: you girls came alone.

They both look at the table, where they are headed.

Earl: Enjoy the night. Tyresha, my offer still stands.

They return to the table.

Bill: Who was that?

Tyresha: My boss.

Bill: Huh! (he looks him over). You want to dance or something to eat.

Tyresha: How about a drink? A martini.

Bill: I want a shot of vodka.

Bill's cell phone goes off. He looks at it but turns it on vibrate.

Tyresha: Whose that?

Bill: Nobody baby. He grabs her and pulls her close.

Tyresha keeps her eyes on Earl.

Bill: What do you do at your new job?

Tyresha: I'm an account executive.

Bill: I'm proud of you.

Lollie is getting sick to her stomach. She and Pierce make out something fierce.

Pierce: Are we going back to my place tonight?

Lollie: If you say so.

Pierce: I'd have it no other way. (nibbles on her ear)

Desiree bust in.

Desiree: Enough you horny toads, only I can do that.

Lollie: Where's your toad?

Desiree: I can't be seen with him, Ed would kill me. He's on his way here now. Oh, hello Bill.

Bill: Hey Desi.

Bill's phone goes off again. He looks at it.
Bill: Baby, can you excuse me one minute.? He walks out and goes outside.
Desiree: You know that's the other woman. You better go and tackle him.
Tyresha: Desi!
Lollie: Look, I don't know what's up with you but you need to drop him and get with the hero. (points at Earl).
Tyresha: Enough, I'm going home. She storms away from the table and makes her way to find Bill.
Overhears.
Bill: Look, I can't keep doing this. Are you okay? How about the baby?
Tyresha stands over him with a glass of wine, she grabbed from the waiter. He turns around only to have the drink poured over him.
Tyresha: So this is what's going on? All that jazz about I love you! (yells, angry) I thought you loved me, but I am just wasting my time.
Bill: Baby, its not like that!!
Tyresha: Go, I want you to pack every piece of garment and get out of my apartment.
She storms off and he grabs her arm.
Bill: Esha, I love you and I wanted to tell you about Violet. I agreed to pay child support, so we can be…
Tyresha: To late. (jerks away).
He follows behind her.
Lollie hears the commotion.
Lollie: Esha!
They rush from the table.
Tyresha rushes to the car. Drops her keys and he picks them up.

Tyresha: Give me my keys!! (takes her heels off to walk faster)
Bill: No, let's talk.
Tyresha: Give me my damn keys!!
Lollie running behind them along with Desiree, Pierce goes along.
Lollie: Esha! You okay.
Bill: This ain't your business Lollie Pop whatever you call yourself.
Tyresha: They were right about you. (crying and reams him out) you are a liar, cheater and a loser. I fought to keep this relationship going. Your treating me like dirt.
Earl goes outside near the club area looking in there direction.
Tyresha: I applaud you for sticking by me, I do. But you never loved me. You never wanted me. You saw a woman who had her own apartment, money and all that jazz. I gave you 100% and I got nothing but a tare of your love. Nothing!!! (tears roll down her cheeks) by this time Lollie and Desiree catch up with her and comfort her.
Tyresha: I hope everything you do falls a part. I HATE YOU!!!
Bill stands there. He is a hard up street fella, who just turned into a wimp over night. He stood there with tears welling up in his eyes.
Desiree drives Tyresha's car home.
Lollie: (to Pierce) Pierce, I'm going…
Pierce nods.
He goes over and kisses her.
They drive off.
Earl watches them drive off.

Moments later.
Tyresha's Apt.

Tyresha sits on the sofa crying, with her make-up running down her cheeks.
Lollie makes some tea.
Desiree: I'm sorry about all of this.
Tyresha: All you ever did was try and tell me about him.
Lollie: We'll stay the night if you want.
She sips her tea and sits Indian style on the sofa looking in a daze.

Next Day.
Lollie and Desi get up to make breakfast.
Tyresha streches.
Lollie: Rise and shine.
They make omelets and pancakes.
Desiree: Get up! breakfast is served.
Lollie: How you feeling?
Tyresha: Better! Thanks you two for staying.
Tyresha looks outside the window and she sees Bill sitting outside talking with Dek.
Lollie: He's been there all morning.
Desiree: I'll help you pack his stuff.
Tyresha: I was so stupid and blind. I saw only what I wanted too.
Lollie: Love does that.
Tyresha: I think I'll be okay.
Desiree: I'm not leaving.
Lollie: I'm hungry.
They sit down to eat.
Tyresha nibbles on her food.
Tyresha exhales in her thoughts of Earl….thoughts dance in her mind. All of a sudden the pain of breaking it off with Bill is over.

Moments Past.

Tyresha lets him in.

Lollie and Desiree sit in the front room.
Bill: Esha, I don't get another chance?
Tyresha: Hell no!!! I forgave you once but this time its over.
He packs his stuff.
Tyresha: Now you can get what you want!…..Her! (with Sarcasm)
Bill grabs his bags. Dek waits for him outside.
Tyresha sees him to the door.
Dek: Hey Esha.
Tyresha: Dek.
They leave.

Later.
Tyresha goes apartment hunting. She drives in front of some townhouses. They are asking $900 a mo. With $900 deposit.
She decides to go and see by appt.
She walks in ,the townhouse has a stainless steel kitchen with a black marble island. The front room is furnished with white and black furniture. It is beyond elegant.

Lady: Do you like it?
Tyresha: I'll take it.
Lady: I can take $900 today and when you move the other $900.
Tyresha: I'll be here in a week.
They finish up with paperwork.

Her cell phone rings. She takes a long drive and ends up at his front door.
He opens the door in a silk biking outfit.
Earl: Come in.
Tyresha: I…(he grabs and kisses her)

They slowly get undressed.
Earl: I wanted you the first time I saw. (almost in a whisper)
He caresses her body slowly. He takes his time with her inch by inch.
They slowly make love for at least an hour. They get in the shower to finish the moment of intimacy.
Later.
They sit down and have a glass of wine. She cuddles up next to him.
Tyresha: I got a new place today.
Earl: Congratulations!
Tyresha: I love it.
Earl: I know this is so soon but, I been wanting to tell you this but….I love you.
Tyresha: You can't really. We just met.
Earl: Not when its real love. I read about your accomplishments, when you were in college. You graduated Cum Laudy. You were in the Business Org Association and you were the President of the Assoc.
Tyresha: You didn't know me then.
Earl: I want to get to know you better if you let me.
Tyresha: I think that can happen.
Earl: I want you to have my babies and be part owner of Bates Brokerage Inc.
Tyresha's mouth drops.

A week later.
Tyresha finishes up her packing to move into her new place.
Desiree and Lollie are in the back room.
A soft knock on the door.
Tyresha wonders who could be knocking on the door.
She opens the door.
Bill: Esha! Can we talk?

She looks back and Desi is peeping from the bedroom door. Tyresha closes the door behind her.

Lollie and Desi peep out the window.

Bill: I want to say I'm sorry about the way I treated you. When, I had you I didn't know what to do with you. I um…made a mistake, why I did it I don't know. They continue to walk.

Bill: I want you to be happy. I wish you the best. I love you and I always will. They stop walking. They look into each other's eye's.

Desiree and Lollie looking through the blinds.

Desiree: She better not kiss that fool.

Lollie: Yes! Kiss him good-bye!!

They look on.

Bill: I wish so much to turn back the hands of time. I got a real job. I am a manager at a paint shop, In a few years, I will own my own company.

Tyresha: What we had was good? I did love you, now, I wish you the best with Violet and the baby.

They have a long kiss goodbye.

They pull a part.

Bill: I will always be here for you. He takes her hand and kisses her index and middle finger.

He walks away.

Tyresha: Bill wait.

She takes off the key to my heart necklace. She gives it to him and walks away.

Tyresha moves into her Town House. She and Earl continue to keep business at the work place and pleasure at home. They continue to date for another year before he proposes to her. She becomes pregnant shortly after with twins. Lollie and Pierce become engaged and still go out to Club Ion. Desiree, well, she is still wild. She and Ed thought about marriage but Desiree likes to get hers. She is not ready to settle down yet but Ed is willing to wait on her.

Bill and Violet continues to live together with their son Micha. Bill is working and making an honest living. But, he can't stop thinking about what might have been between him and Tyresha. Dek and Bill are planning on going partner on the new company. Tyresha drives by the Paint Shop every now and than just to see if Bill is still running a legal business.

She slows down in front of the shop; Bill looks up from putting a finishing touch on a red mustang and sees Tyresha. They both look across at each other and smile. She drives off slowly. Bill continues to look on as she drives off.

Printed in the United States
144694LV00001B/4/P